PROPERTY OF

"It is not what we think or feel that makes us
who we are. It is what we do. Or fail to do . . ."

-SENSE AND SENSIBILITY

DATE _____

DATE _____

DATE

"I HOPE I NEVER RIDICULE
WHAT IS WISE AND GOOD."

—*Pride and Prejudice*

DATE _____

"We have all a better guide in ourselves, if we
would attend to it, than any other person can be."

—MANSFIELD PARK

DATE

DATE _____

"I HAVE NOT WANTED SYLLABLES
WHERE ACTIONS HAVE SPOKEN SO PLAINLY."

—Sense and Sensibility

DATE

"MONEY CAN ONLY GIVE HAPPINESS
WHERE THERE IS NOTHING ELSE TO GIVE IT."

—SENSE AND SENSIBILITY

DATE _____

"IT IS SO DELIGHTFUL TO
HAVE AN EVENING NOW
AND THEN TO ONESELF."

—*Northanger Abbey*

DATE

DATE _____

"I must take care of my mind.
Besides, that would be all recreation and
indulgence, without the wholesome alloy of labour,
and I do not like to eat the bread of idleness."

—MANSFIELD PARK

DATE

DATE _____

DATE _____

"I ALWAYS DESERVE THE BEST
TREATMENT BECAUSE I NEVER
PUT UP WITH ANY OTHER."

—*Emma*

DATE _____

DATE _____

DATE _____

"I am tired of submitting my will
to the caprices of others—of resigning my own
judgement in deference to those to whom I owe
no duty, and for whom I feel no respect. "

—LADY SUSAN

DATE _____

DATE _____

"IF ADVENTURES WILL NOT
BEFALL A YOUNG LADY IN
HER OWN VILLAGE, SHE
MUST SEEK THEM ABROAD."

—*Northanger Abbey*

DATE _____

DATE _____

"I wish, as well as everybody else, to be perfectly
happy; but, like everybody else, it must be in my own way."

—SENSE AND SENSIBILITY

DATE _____

"I AM NOT BORN TO SIT STILL
AND DO NOTHING. IF I LOSE
THE GAME, IT SHALL NOT BE
FROM NOT STRIVING FOR IT. "

—*Mansfield Park*

DATE _____

DATE

"There is a stubbornness about me that never can
bear to be frightened at the will of others. My courage
always rises at every attempt to intimidate me."

—*PRIDE AND PREJUDICE*

"YOU MUST BE THE
BEST JUDGE OF YOUR
OWN HAPPINESS."

—*Emma*

"Everybody likes to go their own way—to
choose their own time and manner of devotion."

—MANSFIELD PARK

DATE _____

"SHE HAD NOTHING TO DO
BUT TO FORGIVE HERSELF
AND BE HAPPIER THAN EVER."

—*Northanger Abbey*

DATE _____

"There will be little rubs and disappointments everywhere, and we are all apt to expect too much; but then, if one scheme of happiness fails, human nature turns to another . . ."

—MANSFIELD PARK

"THINK ONLY OF THE PAST
AS ITS REMEMBRANCE
GIVES YOU PLEASURE."

—*Pride and Prejudice*

"WE NONE OF US EXPECT TO BE
IN SMOOTH WATER ALL OUR DAYS."

—Persuasion

DATE _____